©2025 Nikolette Kelson

All rights reserved. Published by Scholastic Inc., *Publishers since 1920*. SCHOLASTIC and associated logos are trademarks and/or registered trademarks of Scholastic Inc.

The publisher does not have any control over and does not assume any responsibility for author or third-party websites or their content.

No part of this publication may be reproduced, stored in a retrieval system, or transmitted in any form or by any means, electronic, mechanical, photocopying, recording, or otherwise, or used to train any artificial intelligence technologies, without written permission of the publisher. For information regarding permission, write to Scholastic Inc., Attention: Permissions Department, 557 Broadway, New York, NY 10012.

This book is a work of fiction. Names, characters, places, and incidents are either the product of the author's imagination or are used fictitiously, and any resemblance to actual persons, living or dead, business establishments, events, or locales is entirely coincidental.

ISBN 978-1-338-79240-9

10 9 8 7 6 5 4 3 2 1   25 26 27 28 29

Printed in China   38

First printing 2025

Illustrations by Elle Pierre and Anastasiia Drakova

Book design by Martha Maynard and Katie Fitch

We all have a rainbow inside, and it's made up of all the special little things that make each of us unique.

Everyone's rainbow looks **a little different**. I know mine does! But that's one of the best parts about being **human**.

There were times when I was afraid to be **honest** about what I liked.

Expressing yourself can be scary.

But talking to my friends about my feelings made everything better!

No matter how hard I tried, I could not hide my **rainbow** or my love for **unicorns**.

So I decided to **embrace it!**

Sometimes I snort when I laugh really hard...

I used to be **embarrassed**, but now I don't even think about it!

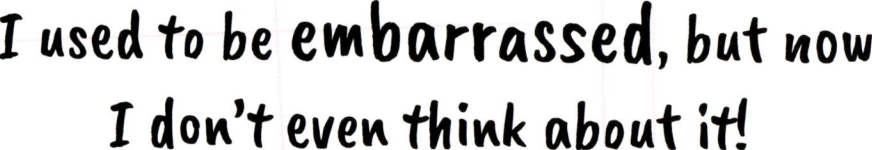

Some people think I'm a little too much, but I don't care, because I know **I'm just right.**

Whenever I wear an outfit that makes me feel **happy**...

. . . or braid my hair the way I like, my rainbow grows and glows.

Every time I feel the groove and start **dancing**,

But my rainbow isn't just about what I do, it's about who and what I am.

Whenever the fear comes back
and I want to stay inside...

I just focus on being myself and live in the moment.

Now whatever it is I'm **feeling**, I don't try to hide it.

I'm excited to skate... I was just feeling really nervous about going out.

So, how do you share your rainbow with the world? Don't be shy. Let your rainbow **shine bright** just like me!

JADE

AMINA